HOW LOUD CAN A DRAGONFLY ROAR?

TIFFANY ROOT
(WITH KAYLEE ROOT)

ASSOCIATION OF INSECT RESEARCHERS

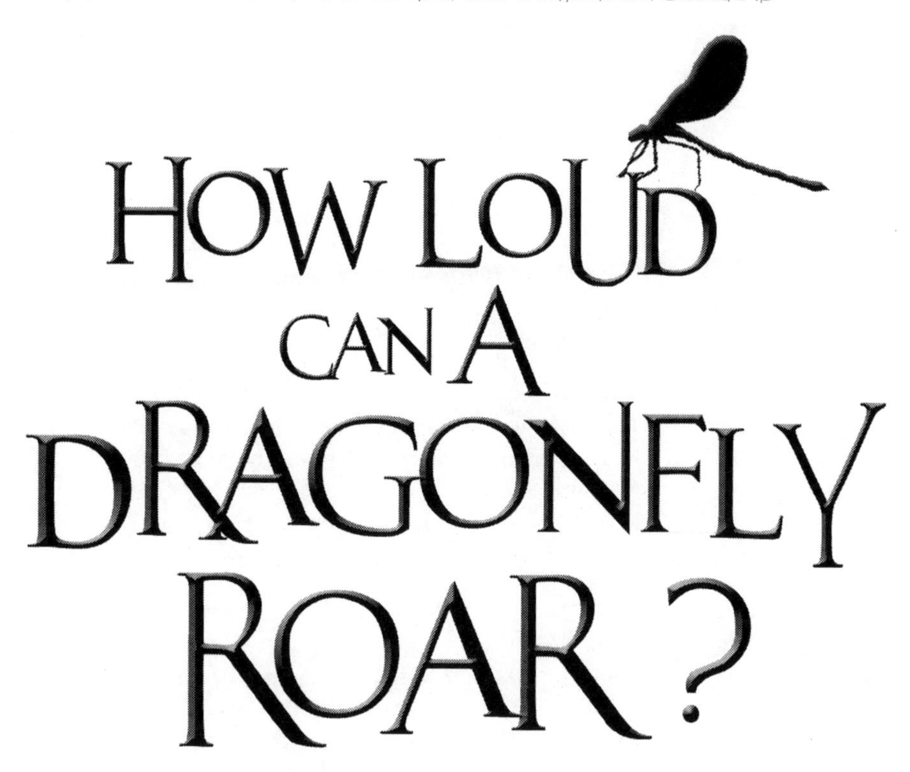

ILLUSTRATED BY

KATE THRAMS

TATE PUBLISHING
AND ENTERPRISES, LLC

How Loud Can a Dragonfly Roar?
Copyright © 2013 by Tiffany Root. All rights reserved.

No part of this publication may be reproduced, stored in a retrieval system or transmitted in any way by any means, electronic, mechanical, photocopy, recording or otherwise without the prior permission of the author except as provided by USA copyright law.

This novel is a work of fiction. Names, descriptions, entities, and incidents included in the story are products of the author's imagination. Any resemblance to actual persons, events, and entities is entirely coincidental.

The opinions expressed by the author are not necessarily those of Tate Publishing, LLC.

Published by Tate Publishing & Enterprises, LLC
127 E. Trade Center Terrace | Mustang, Oklahoma 73064 USA
1.888.361.9473 | www.tatepublishing.com

Tate Publishing is committed to excellence in the publishing industry. The company reflects the philosophy established by the founders, based on Psalm 68:11,
"The Lord gave the word and great was the company of those who published it."

Book design copyright © 2013 by Tate Publishing, LLC. All rights reserved.
Cover design by Joseph Emnace
Interior design by Gram Telen
Illustrations by Kate Thrams

Published in the United States of America

ISBN: 978-1-62994-138-7
1. Juvenile Fiction / Animals / Insects, Spiders, etc.
2. Juvenile Fiction / People & Places / Africa
13.11.07

DEDICATION

This book is dedicated to my son, William, whose dream it is to go to Africa. William, may the Lord bless you and fill you to overflowing with His great love. May you know His heart and bring glory to His great name.

TABLE OF CONTENTS

CHAPTER 1

ASSOCIATION OF INSECT RESEARCHERS

The sun was bright over the Grand River as Mr. Beetle arrived with his briefcase and spectacles. Mumbling to himself, he hurried to the dock over the fish ladder. Several people were watching the fish jump up the ladder.

One girl, about the age of eight, was squealing in delight as she cheered on one particular salmon in her journey up the ladder. Her brother, a blond-haired, blue-eyed five-year-old, yelled at his salmon of choice to jump faster. Their other sibling, a cute, curly-haired brunette, was not watching the fish, but instead seemed interested in something going on in the corner of the dock. It happened to be the entryway that Mr. Beetle needed to access.

The little girl had become interested in all the bugs entering through that particular hole. She wasn't brave enough yet to touch the bugs, but he didn't want her to catch the attention of her father, who may realize something was going on.

Mr. Beetle thought quickly. He caught the attention of a dragonfly overhead and motioned for it to come near. The dragonfly quickly dropped down next to Mr. Beetle within hearing range.

"How can I help you, sir?" the dragonfly asked, his bright blue-and-green wings fluttering as he held himself slightly above Mr. Beetle.

"We have a problem, Mike," said Mr. Beetle. "I need you to distract the human girl so we can get into the meeting safely."

"Roger that, Mr. Beetle. I'm on it!" responded Mike as he buzzed away.

Mike buzzed toward the little girl, and just as it looked like he would smack right into her face, he pulled up and went right over her head. The distraction worked! The girl looked up and turned around, trying to see what had almost hit her. That's when Mike came back and started flying in circles around her.

Dragonflies are notoriously fast flyers, and the little girl forgot all about the many bugs filing into the hole in the ground as she watched Mike fly around her. Instead she became consumed with trying to catch the dragonfly that zoomed around her head.

"Daddy, look!" she cried. "A big fly, like a butterfly. I want to catch it."

Hearing those words, Mike decided to leave the area for a bit until the coast was clear and he could get into the entryway of the meeting himself without being noticed.

It took a few more minutes before the father and the three children left. Only a few people were left on the dock when Mike flew back in.

"Perfect," he said to himself. Lowering down closer, he buzzed into the hole. Dragonflies cannot walk well, so he had to fly into the hole, watching to make sure his wide wings did not hit the sides of the walls.

Voices greeted him as he flew down the earthen stairway into the meeting area under the dock. It was the meeting of the Association of Insect Researchers, or AIR for short. Here is where all the leaders in the various fields of research meet twice each year to determine the areas needing to be researched and who is best qualified to do the work. Insects from around the world gather in the early spring and fall under the dock overlooking the fish ladder in the Grand River of Grand Rapids, Michigan.

Sometimes in the early spring there is a lot of snow and ice, but this year the weather was warm, and the spring rains had not yet started to cause flooding and other dangers to the insects. The room they met in was large with spacious chairs for the larger insects like cockroaches and those with wings, like Mike and the other dragonflies, as well as butterflies. The chairs formed a U centering on the platform Mr. Beetle was standing on while he surveyed the crowd. A flashlight hung from the ceiling, giving light to the many insects rustling papers and chatting with friends they had not seen since fall.

Mike found a seat next to the only other dragonflies in the crowd. Dora had the best memory of anyone Mike knew. She remembered facts as if she were a walking encyclopedia. Her transparent green, reflective wings beat excitedly as she explained to her friend Lydia the new discoveries she had made in studying pond slime. Lydia, a beautiful dragonfly with purple and blue hues, nodded patiently and kindly. She was known for her sweet demeanor and ability to recognize the needs of others.

Mike perched next to Lydia and was about to ask Dora a question regarding her recent studies, when he was interrupted by a rapping on the podium.

"Attention members of AIR," Mr. Beetle loudly proclaimed. "Welcome to the annual spring meeting of the Association of Insect Researchers. I hope that you grabbed your bi-yearly report as you walked in the door. Today we have several items on the agenda. As you feel the desire to volunteer to research the various needs that arise, please raise your hand, and we will assign duties that way."

The meeting commenced, and various insects were assigned various places to study many different things, like space travel, monkeys in Peru, Beluga whales, and more. Lulu Ladybug, sitting in front of Mike, got assigned to study what to do about the Asian Carp in the Great Lakes.

"Excuse me," came a very small, high-pitched voice.

“Yes?” said Mr. Beetle, looking around.

“Over here!” came the voice. “I’m over here to your left and on the end!”

“Oh yes, so sorry I didn’t see you, Bob Fireant.” Mr. Beetle smiled graciously. “Please go ahead.”

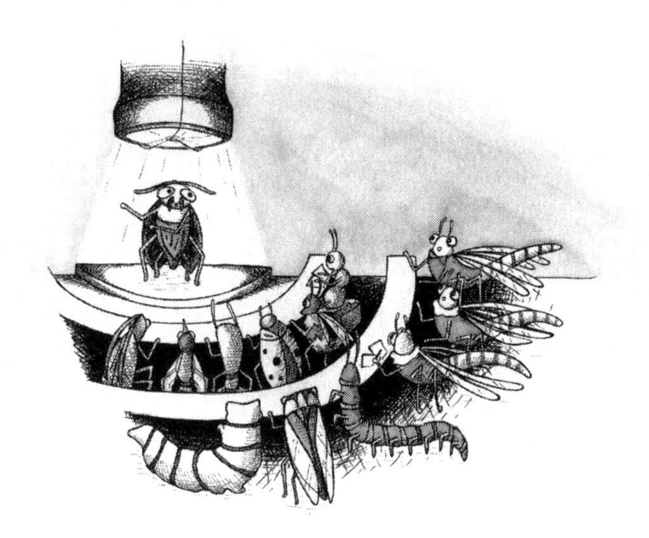

Bob spoke as loudly as he could, but everyone still strained to hear him. “It’s my understanding,” he started, “that the lion in the city zoo in Cleveland, where I am from, has died.”

He coughed and continued. “My concern is that I have no idea, nor do my fellow insects that I have spoken to, how many lions there are left in this world. Maybe they are endangered and we need to do something to save them. Maybe there are too many and we need to make reforms. Maybe we need to protect their habitats. I just don’t know. Therefore, I propose that a group of delegates be sent to Africa to gather information and report back to us in the fall." Bob smiled, nodded, and sat back down.

Mr. Beetle thought for a moment and then said, "Well, is there anyone willing to go?"

Mike was about bursting at his wings. Go to Africa and study lions? Of course he wanted to go.

But before he could raise his hand, Dora was already fluttering above her seat and yelling, "Oh, sir, please, I would like to go!"

"Fine, fine, Dora Dragonfly," said Mr. Beetle. "You may go. Please choose one or two others to help you."

Dora looked over at Mike and Lydia. "Well, what do you think?" she asked. "Do you want to go?"

"Do I ever!" exclaimed Mike.

"Me too." Lydia smiled. "I'd love to go."

And so the preparations for Africa began.

CHAPTER 2

THE JOURNEY BEGINS

"There's a train headed for Myrtle Beach, South Carolina, at 11:00 p.m. tonight," called Mike from the study in a tidy little house located in the large maple tree next to a pond in Riverside Park.

"That hardly gives us any time," replied Dora. "No, look for a train going first thing in the morning."

"Okay, okay," mumbled Mike. He did some more typing on his miniature computer. The internet connection flickered, and Mike grumbled. One of the houses located across the park from Mike's tree gave good internet connection to Mike, but sometimes because of the tiny size of Mike's computer, there were glitches.

"Finally!" he said, grinning. "Holden Beach, North Carolina. It leaves at 5:00 a.m. from Grand Rapids, and it arrives at our destination at precisely one in the morning."

"Perfect." Lydia smiled. "Let's get our stuff together. Dora and I will go home and pack. We'll meet you at the train station at four thirty."

"See you then!" Mike waved.

SUBWAY TIME

Zoom! A train sped past Dora, causing her antennas to blow wildly.

"You have the tickets?" she asked Mike for the third time.

"Yes," he replied, trying not to sound irritated. "I *still* have them."

"Okay, you two," Lydia sweetly interrupted. "This one's ours."

They quickly climbed aboard, trying not to bump the other insects with their backpacks. Some bugs could sit four to a bench on the train, but because of their wings, Mike, Dora, and Lydia had to sit two to a bench. Well, they called it "sitting," but it was actually perching on the back of a bench or chair by holding on with their feet.

Mike sat by himself at the back of the car, while Lydia and Dora found a bench at the front. They settled down for what was going to be a long ride. Facing them sat a ladybug that Lydia recognized from the AIR meeting the day before.

"How do you do?" the ladybug politely inquired of Dora and Lydia.

"Very well," Lydia responded. "And are you on your way home?"

"Yes," he drawled. "I'm from North Carolina. And you?"

"Oh, we're from Michigan, but we're on our way to North Carolina. Then we have to take a ship to Africa. We've been given the opportunity to study lions."

"Oh my," he smiled. "That sounds like a wonderful adventure. I just finished a study on humans. It took me three years."

"Really?" Dora questioned. "Please tell us what you've learned. It will make this ride so much more interesting."

Lydia glanced at Mike, who was doing his best to fall asleep as the ladybug from the South started his talk on humans.

ON THE WATER

The train came to a slow halt, and Mike stretched his shoulders, causing his wings to flutter briefly. He was glad to be able to get off the train and fly around a bit before embarking on the ship that would take them to another continent.

He watched Dora and Lydia hug a male ladybug good-bye, and he made his way over to them. The doors to the train opened before they could say anything, so he waited until they were outside the station to discuss their next moves.

"Oh, Mike!" exclaimed Lydia. "We've just heard the most fascinating information about humans from Mr. Spotter. He's such a nice gentlebug from North Carolina. We'll tell you everything we've learned on the boat. Let's go!"

"And they all speak different languages everywhere you go, just like insects!" Dora said, finishing her discourse on humans as they approached the enormous black ship that would take them to Africa.

The three dragonflies fluttered about with their backpacks as they tried to avoid being stepped on or swatted by humans.

"Where's the door?" questioned Lydia.

"Oh, oh, over there!" exclaimed Dora, pointing to a small window toward the bottom of the ship.

A large black, hairy spider was perched outside the window taking tickets in one hand and assisting the oncoming bugs with another hand while he held onto the ship with his legs.

"Hello, Mr. Spider," said Lydia cheerfully as she approached him with Mike and Dora following.

"Oh, hello," he said in a much gentler voice than his fierce appearance would lead one to believe him capable of. "Name's Bill. Tickets, please."

Mike fluttered in front of the two ladies and handed the spider all three tickets.

"Right through here and to your left you will find cabin number seven, which is yours," said the spider named Bill as he reached for the next ticket.

The three dragonflies found their room and got settled in. After unpacking, they decided to go exploring. They saw a sign that said "Hold" where a man was entering.

"That looks like a good place to explore," said Dora.

"I don't know," Mike replied. "I'd rather go up to the top and smell the salty air."

"Well, we really should stay together," said Lydia. The blue on her wing tips flashed in the dim light as she showed her concern.

"Mike, let's just go in the *hold*, whatever that is," said Dora, "and then we can go up to the top."

"Oh, all right," Mike sighed. "I hope I get to make some of the decisions this trip," he grumbled.

The trio perched on top of the doorway and waited for someone to open the door. After a few minutes, a man came out, and Dora and Lydia quickly flew in. Mike almost made it, but the door shut too quickly. He winced as the wind from the shutting door lifted his wings high into the air.

"Well, the hold looks good," said the man who had exited. "I won't need to go in there until we dock in Africa," he continued to himself.

"Oh no!" Mike yelled. "They're going to be stuck in there until we arrive in Africa. I knew they should have listened to me. What am I going to do now?" he asked frantically.

"Okay, okay, okay. Now, I've been trained in this sort of thing. I just need to be calm and figure something out." He flew back and forth across the door thinking, thinking, thinking. Suddenly, it came to him!

"Pray! Of course!" Mike yelled excitedly. "James 1 says that if we ask for wisdom, God will give it to us. So, I'll ask for wisdom."

"Oh God," Mike began, "Lydia and Dora are stuck in the hold. Please give me wisdom to get them out."

He waited. Suddenly the idea to pray for someone to come and open the door came to him. He knew he hadn't thought of that idea himself. It was from God. He had gotten wisdom on how to pray!

"Amazing," he whispered. "Okay, God, please send someone back to open the door."

"One more box," came a voice down the hall. "Why can't people check in their boxes in a timely manner?"

It was the same man who a few minutes before had said he wouldn't be back to the hold until they docked in Africa! Mike was beside himself with joy as the man unlocked the door and entered in. Mike followed quickly behind him, whispering a prayer of thanks.

"Dora, Lydia!" he yelled. "Quickly, come to the entrance!"

"Mike," said Lydia sweetly, "we've been waiting right here since we noticed you had not followed us in. You don't have to yell."

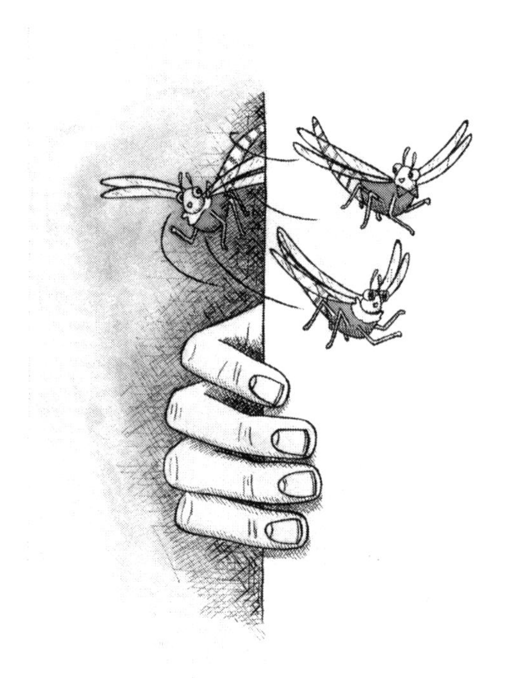

"Oh," Mike sighed with relief. "We've got to follow this guy out when he opens the door to leave or we'll be stuck in here the whole trip to Africa."

"Oh dear," Lydia said. "That would be horrible."

"Dreadfully so," agreed Dora as the man came back and opened the door to exit.

This time all three made it through the door before it shut and locked again.

That night was a sweet night of rest for all three dragonflies as they thanked God for sparing them from a dreadful trip to Africa stuck in a hold.

CHAPTER 3

AFRICA

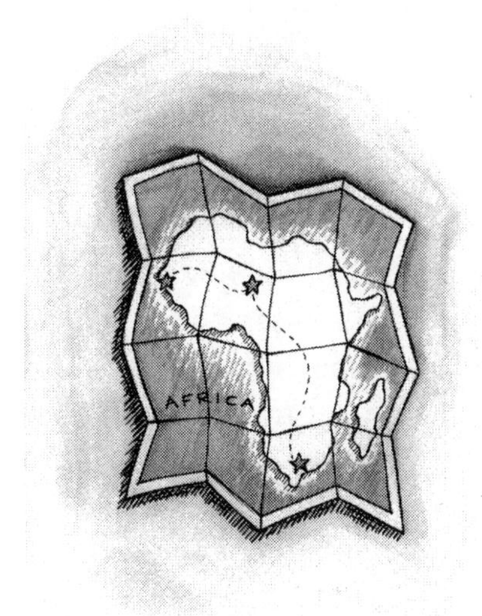

"Land ho!" yelled a sailor on deck.

"Oh, Mike!" cried Lydia. "We're there!"

Mike was getting his breath of fresh salty air for the day when land was spotted by the human crew on board the ship. Lydia and Dora were with him, not wanting to be separated again after almost getting locked in the hold.

"Oh, thank God," said Dora, sighing with relief. "This has been a long ride. I've hardly slept at all, what with all the rocking of the boat. At least I had plenty of time to think of and write down questions we want answered on this mission."

"Thanks for doing that, Dora," said Mike. "That will save us a lot of time when we finally find a *pride* of lions to study."

"What's a pride?" questioned Lydia.

"A pride is a group of lions that are usually related," responded Dora. She had brought all the information the insect kingdom knew about lions and had been studying it the entire week they had been on the barge.

"Well, I learned something already," said Lydia. "A pride. What a delightful name for a family."

The three friends had to go back down off the deck and disembark through the same window in which they entered so that the spider could keep record of every bug that came on and off the barge. Exiting through the window, they took a deep breath and flew to the nearest tree to discuss their next move.

"Where are we anyway?" asked Lydia, blinking from the hot sun.

"We are in Mauritania," answered Dora while looking through a map that she had brought.

"Let me see that," said Mike, grabbing for the map.

"Well, I'm the one who remembered to bring it," Dora said, holding it above her head.

"Hey, you two," interrupted Lydia. "Let's not fight. Dora, do you mind if Mike leads us? He's very good at finding his way."

"Oh, all right," said Dora. "Here." And she handed the map to Mike.

Smiling in thanks, he opened it and pointed to where they were. "We have to get to Niger."

"Why Niger?" asked Lydia.

"Well, we have to go somewhere. I don't see any lions here in Mauritania. So, let's find a train."

Buzzzzzzzzzz. A mosquito landed next to Mike on the tree branch.

"Hey, I haven't seen you around these parts before. Are you visiting?" asked the Mosquito, who seemed unusually large compared to the mosquitoes in Michigan.

"Well, yes," answered Mike. "We just arrived in Africa."

"We're looking for a train that can take us to Niger," added Dora. "Do you know where we can find one?"

"Do I? You've met the right guide here. Why, I know everything about these parts," he said, buzzing back and forth in front of the AIR members.

"Do you know if there are any lions here?" asked Lydia.

"No, no," answered the mosquito. "Don't you worry about that, pretty lady. There are no lions around these parts."

Before any of the dragonflies could answer and tell him they wanted to see lions, the mosquito just kept on talking. Turns out he was quite the talker indeed. In fact, he talked nonstop all the way to the train station.

"Well, here we are," he announced when they arrived at the depot. "Have a great time in Africa, and I sure hope you don't meet any lions."

"Thank you," each dragonfly replied.

"Well," said Mike, after the mosquito left, "he talked so much, we never even learned his name. Besides that, I hope he's wrong and we do find some lions, since that's the reason we came all the way here."

"No kidding," said Dora, smiling.

They approached the ticket counter, which was cleverly situated underneath the crevice of a rock, hidden from view of the humans. Mike purchased three tickets to Niger, three snack bags, and some pond water to drink. His hands were full, and he flew low and slow so as not to drop anything.

"Thank you so much," said Lydia, taking the drink and snacks from him.

"We better get going," said Dora matter-of-factly. "We don't want to miss the train. It leaves in just a few minutes."

They each grabbed their gear and headed back under the rock where the train was located. Handing their tickets to the conductor, who happened to be a large black fly with a grim expression, they found seats and settled in for the ride.

"We should be there by late tomorrow or early the next day," said Dora, doing the calculations of miles and speed on her calculator.

"Well, I hope this food fills us up until we see sunlight again then," said Mike, breaking into his snack bag.

"It's too bad we can't see the sunlight until we arrive," answered Lydia. "This train travel underground is so gloomy."

"But at least we're safe here from humans and others who may step on us," answered Dora, yawning and waving her hand. "And now I think I'll take a nap." She closed her eyes and was sleeping before the train even departed the station.

Screeeeeech!

The train came to a halt, and Dora jerked awake.

"Whoa!" she said. "Are we there already?"

"I would say so," answered Lydia. "You slept the entire trip!"

"Wow, I guess I was tired."

Stumbling into the sunlight after being in the dark tunnel for so long, they were amazed to see so many bugs. There were termites everywhere, or so it seemed. There were plenty of other bugs too, but the termites far outnumbered any other insect.

"What is this place?" said Lydia, looking around.

"Well, it's Niger, I guess," responded Mike.

"You don't look like you're from around here," said a large termite, twice the size of Mike. "Do you three need help finding where to go?"

"Oh, yes," said Lydia. "We are in Niger, right?"

"Niger? Absolutely!" boomed the big termite. "Name's Bob. Where in Niger do ya plan to go?"

"Oh anywhere there are lions!" broke in Mike.

"Lions! Oh no, my friend. There are no lions here."

The three dragonflies looked at each other. Their shoulders drooped, and they sighed.

"What now?" grumbled Mike. "What do we do now?"

CHAPTER 4

TERMITE FRIENDS

"If you don't mind me asking," said the large termite named Bob, "What in the world do you want to see lions for anyway? They's not that exciting, ya know, and if you get in their way, they's likely to snip ya's up with they big teeth."

Big tears started to well up in Lydia's eyes as she took in this new information. Bravely, she held them at bay and bit her lip to keep it from quivering.

"Oh dear, oh dear," said Dora. "Well, let's not fret," she continued, trying to calm herself as well as Mike and Lydia. "There *are* lions in Africa. We just have to figure out where. I know we're tired, but there are approximately sixteen thousand to forty-seven thousand lions in Africa, depending on which source one reads. We've got to encounter a lion with that many around."

"Bob," interjected Mike. "Would you be so kind as to tell us where we can find lions in Africa?"

"Well, my friend, your best bet would be to visit Kruger National Park in South Africa. They's about two thousand lions just in that one place."

"South Africa!" exclaimed Dora. "That's about 3,475 miles away, give or take a few miles."

"Oh, don't you worry, friends. Come with me."

And with that the big termite started across the sand headed east. Mike shrugged at the ladies and followed after Bob. Lydia and Dora hurried to catch up.

They had only traveled about ten minutes when they approached what seemed to be a small mountain made of dirt, standing about twenty feet tall.

"This is my home," said Bob, pointing at the structure.

"You live here by yourself?" said Mike incredulously.

"Oh no," Bob laughed. "I share it with about five million of my close family members. My mom is the queen, and my dad is the king. I'll introduce you when we get inside."

A guard stood at the entryway. "Halt. Who goes there?" he boomed.

"It's me, Bob."

"Who's that with you? Spies?" he asked, peering suspiciously at Mike, Lydia, and Dora.

Lydia shuddered at the interrogating stare of the termite guard, and her wings shook.

Bob laughed. "No, my friend, not spies. I'm going to introduce them to Mom and Dad. They's need some help. They's visiting all the way from the United States of America."

"That so," said the guard. "Well, then right inside. Stick together, and don't disrupt the workers."

The inside of the mound was about 84 to 86 degrees. Dora was busily taking notes regarding everything they saw. Mike flew behind the girls, feeling as though he needed to protect them, just in case of what, he didn't know. Thankfully the termites were so large that their tunnels were also large, making room for the large wings of the dragonflies.

They traveled through many tunnels and past many different chambers. Some chambers held eggs, some held baby termites, and many held food.

Finally, they arrived at a chamber protected by four armed guards. They heard the familiar "Halt. Who goes there?" when they arrived.

Mike explained their situation and asked to see the king and queen. One guard entered into the chamber to ask permission, and Dora quickly sketched a picture of the guards while they waited.

"Okay," the guard said. "You may enter. Keep in mind you are approaching royalty. Please act appropriately."

"Yes, sir," said Mike.

"Come on," said Bob, motioning them inside. "And don't worry. Mom and Dad are great. You don't have to be nervous."

Inside sat a male and female termite being fanned by attendants, who were using large leaves to keep them cool. Mike, Lydia, and Dora bowed, and Bob walked up and hugged each parent.

"Thank you for taking the time to meet with us," said Bob to his parents. "We'll try to be brief."

"Yes, Bob," said the king. "Your mother lays about thirty thousand eggs a day, so we really can't take too many breaks."

"Thirty thousand eggs!" exclaimed Dora. "Couldn't you get someone else to lay eggs too, Your Majesty?"

The queen smiled sweetly, showing perfectly white teeth. "No, my dear. Then all these wonderful termites you see in the mound would not be my children. They would belong to someone else."

"You mean every termite here is your child?" said Lydia, mouth agape. "How do you parent them all?"

"Oh, each child gets time alone with us at least once a year, and sometimes more, such as in this case," answered the queen, looking at Bob.

"Yes, and of course every child knows he or she is loved," added the king, squeezing his wife's hand. "So, what can we do for you?"

"Well, sir," said Mike, taking the lead. "We have come on a mission by way of the Association of Insect Researchers. We're based out of the United States, and our mission is to study lions. We've gotten this far, and now we need to get to where there are lions. Bob indicated there were some in South Africa, but we do not know how to go about getting there."

"Yes," interjected Bob. "And I thought perhaps we could help them. George and Willie have that airplane, and if it's not in use at the moment, could our new friends use it?"

"Why, of course," said the queen. "I don't see why not."

"Me either," added the king. "Be blessed, and may your mission be a success."

"Oh, thank you," said Lydia, forgetting protocol and flying to hug the king and queen.

The startled guards didn't even have time to stop her, but there was no need. The queen and king were happy for the hug, and then they were on their way to find George and Willie.

George and Willie were in a room close to the back exit working on a helicopter. The helicopter looked as though it had been a human child's toy before.

"Hope our plane isn't a toy," mumbled Mike.

He spoke too soon, for indeed the airplane they were to ride on for thirty-five hours was a toy airplane. However, the termites were geniuses as far as bugs go. They had figured out a way to get the plane to actually fly. It was quite large for a toy, and the three dragonflies fit nicely inside with their laptop and backpacks. The pilot and co-pilot had ample room in the front of the plane too. The termites even employed a young termite male named Jeremy to come with them and see to their needs. It didn't hurt that he was also a mechanic should anything go wrong.

"Before you go," said Bob as they approached the ladder to the plane, "I hope ya don't mind if we say a prayer for a safe trip and successful mission."

"Mind?" asked Dora. "We'd be so very grateful."

The three dragonflies and the four termites knelt to the ground and prayed to the God of heaven and earth to protect the airplane and its passengers and to grant the dragonflies success on their mission. With hugs all around, they boarded the plane, except Bob, who stood below waving and smiling.

CHAPTER 5

THE TAMBOTI TREE

Dora, Mike, and Lydia settled down for the long flight. Jeremy turned out to be a most gracious assistant on the plane. He made sure they had enough drinks of sugar water and food to eat. He also checked with them regularly to be sure they were each comfortable. The pilots were also very attentive to their flying passengers, making sure to inform them of their whereabouts and altitude at various intervals.

For her part Dora spent the time on the plane researching lions. She shared much useful information with Mike and Lydia.

"Did you know that there should be a *dominant* male in each pride? That's going to be the lion that is in charge of a group of lions that live together," she told Mike and Lydia.

"Well, that makes sense," said Mike. "I guess I'd be the dominant male of our little trio." He laughed, amused with his own humor.

"I suppose if you were a lion and we were lionesses, that might be the case, but don't bet on being the leader," countered Dora.

Lydia chuckled. "Well, I've no inclination at all to be the leader, so you two can just fight it out!"

They all laughed, knowing that they were a team and each would lead as needed.

They were interrupted as the pilot announced, "We've just crossed the border into South Africa. This, my friends, is your destination. We'll be in Kruger National Park shortly. Keep a close eye out the window, and let me know when you see a spot to land. My recommendation would be, of course, to make sure there are lions present before landing."

Jeremy started cleaning up the cabin of the plane as the dragonfly trio eagerly swept their eyes up and down the African plains looking for lions.

It was about a half hour later when they spotted a few lions.

"Fly down closer!" yelled Mike. "I see some!"

The pilot swooped down to have a closer look.

"Oh, no!" exclaimed Dora disappointedly. "Those are a group of males. I don't see any females or cubs at all. I think to do our job best we better make sure we study all types of lions, not just males."

"Yes," said Lydia, fluttering her wings slightly. "That sounds very sensible, Dora."

The pilot took the plane back up, and they kept flying. It was another half an hour before they finally found another pride. This time it was just what they were looking for.

"Oooohhhh!" exclaimed Lydia. "I count at least eight lions and several cubs."

"This is just what we need," said Mike. "Now, where do we land and set up camp?" His eyebrows furrowed in thought.

"Well," Jeremy said, interrupting his thoughts. "May I suggest we land you near a tree? That way you will have opportunity to fly higher and perch. From that viewpoint you will be able to better see the lions."

"Of course!" retorted Mike. "We need to be by a tree."

"Wait!" interrupted Dora. "Lions climb trees. We don't really want to be in a tree and have a lion come too close, you know?"

"Oh dear," said Lydia.

"Yeah, but we should be up high for a better view," said Mike.

"Let me do some quick research on the trees in the area and see if I can come up with anything," responded Dora. Biting her underlip in concentration, she started searching on her laptop. It didn't take long before she broke into a grin and looked up at the rest of the bugs in the plane, who were anxiously awaiting their next move.

"We need to find a Tamboti tree," she said excitedly, her antennas twitching in excitement. "Tamboti trees are *deciduous*, of medium height, and the milky latex they produce can cause severe irritation to the skin and eyes. I believe lions will not climb these trees as they do other ones because of it."

"Perfect!" Lydia laughed. "Just perfect."

"Lead the way," said the pilot, sighing with relief.

"Head north a little, and we'll see if we can spot one," replied Dora.

They spotted one within a few minutes and safely landed only about a football field away from where the pride was lying in the grass. The pilot did a magnificent job maneuvering the plane to land almost right next to the trunk of the Tamboti tree.

After Jeremy unloaded their luggage and helped them carry it up safely into the tree, the three termites were on their way.

Lydia blinked back tears as they left. "Oh, I do hope we see them again," she said.

"Don't worry," said Mike. "They told us we can get word to them to pick us back up for the ride home. I'm sure they're right. We just have to find termites around here, and they'll spread the word when our study is done."

After unpacking and setting up a shelter in a dip in one of the uppermost tree branches, the three friends decided to fly down for a closer look and see what they could learn before the sun went down for the night.

The three dragonflies buzzed quietly over the resting pride. "Why are they all just lying there?" asked Lydia. "Don't lions hunt?"

"Well," stated Dora. "They hunt, but only at night when it's cooler. We should see some action fairly soon."

"Let's see if we can figure out who the dominant male is and maybe some names," said Mike.

The three friends landed in the grass and watched the pride. There were two male adults and six female adults. The dragonflies counted nine cubs of varying ages. The cubs were tackling each other and chasing the tales of the lionesses and the two male lions. Dora was writing in her notebook these basic facts when they observed one of the males stand up. All the lions looked up at him as he stood. He shook his mane and started walking away from the pride. Soon, the three dragonflies observed him scratching trees and rubbing his *scent* on large boundary trees and stones around the pride.

"I'm going to follow him," said Mike.

When Mike and the lion returned, Mike reported what he had learned.

"Not only did he rub his scent and scratch up trees, but he urinated in various places as he walked what seemed to be the boundary lines of his pride."

"Very interesting," said Dora. "I venture to guess he is the dominant male, and he is leaving his scent as a warning to other lions so they do not come too close."

Dora's guess proved to be right. When Dora, Lydia, and Mike returned to their Tamboti tree house, they discussed what they learned and decided to give names to the lions so they would know who they were talking about. They placed the names and descriptions in a chart similar to the one below.

Dominant Male	Jones	Large male lion with a darker-colored mane
2nd in Command Male	Hunter	Large male lion with slightly lighter coloring in his mane than Jones.
1st Female – Leader	Africa	Large lioness with two cubs, who seems to be the leader of the females. CUBS: Henry (male) Becca (female)
2nd Female	Cassandra	No cubs, seems pregnant
3rd Female	Lia	Four cubs CUBS: Kitty (female) Pounce (male) Springer (male) Chubs (male)
4th Female	Rachel	No cubs, seems pregnant
5th Female	Polly	Three cubs CUBS: Fuzzy (male) Sparkle (female) Cuddles (female)
6th Female	Suzie	No cubs

After filling out their journal, the three dragonflies relaxed their wings as they perched quietly on a branch and quickly fell asleep. Tomorrow would be a big day, and they were tired from their long journey across the world.

CHAPTER 6

HABITAT OF THE TRIBE

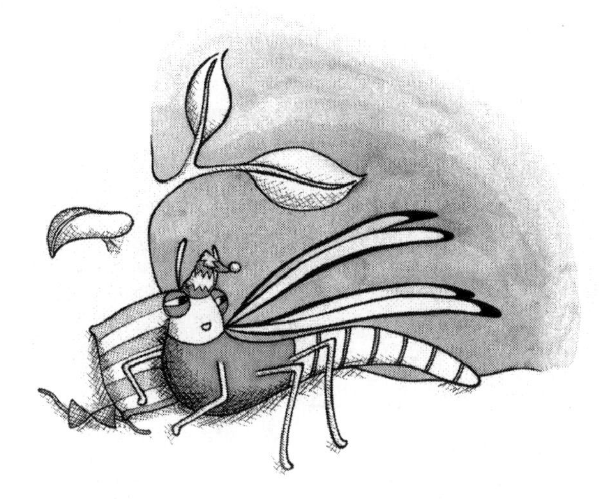

"Rise and shine," said Lydia brightly, shaking the other two slumbering dragonflies. "It's a beautiful day, and we need to get busy!"

Mike turned his head and grumbled something under his breath.

"Already?" said Dora, stretching her wings and yawning loudly. "I think I could have slept until tomorrow!"

"I've got breakfast ready," said Lydia, ignoring the complaints.

"Thank you," Dora smiled. "Sorry I slept in. I'll get right up and get us ready."

Mike slowly fluttered his wings and flew up in the air for a stretch. "I guess I'll get up too. No doubt the two of you won't let me sleep any longer."

"No doubt, indeed," replied Lydia.

"Okay," said Dora after they had finished their breakfast. "Let's start by studying the habitat of the lions so we are familiar with the environment best suited for lions."

"That sounds like a smart idea," said Lydia.

"I thought we were supposed to find out how many lions there are and stuff like that," said Mike.

"Well, that is certainly one thing we need to make sure of. However, I actually found those statistics already under some studies humans have done on lions. I think our best use of time would be to have a hands-on study of a particular pride, like this one, that could be indicative of almost all other prides. That would be a report that the AIR would appreciate," responded Dora.

Mike shrugged. "I guess."

And they were off. They circled the territory of the pride they were observing and stopped frequently to take notes.

The first thing they noticed about their environment was how warm it was. Stopping to rest on a tree branch to draw a picture of their surroundings, they asked a fly if the warmth continued all year.

"Oh, yes," buzzed the fly. "Oh yes, oh yes. It's warm all year. Right nice it is. But I must say," he continued. "It's not rainy all year. No, no, no. Not rainy all year. You've come at a good time. It's the end of the rainy season, so everything is lush and green."

"Thank you," responded Mike. "You've been a big help."

"Okay," said Dora. "So we know that it's warm all year in the African Savannah, and there is a rainy season that we've missed, thankfully."

"What's a savannah?" asked Lydia.

"A *savannah* is a grassland," responded Dora. "That's where we are right now. We're in a grassland."

"Of course." Lydia smiled brightly. "A perfect place for animals that eat grass, like zebras and giraffes."

"And a perfect place for animals that like to eat grass-eating animals." Mike chuckled.

"So, what else do we know?" questioned Lydia.

"Well," began Dora, "We know that the lions live among the trees and bushes. They seem to rest during the day and hunt at night when their vision is excellent. We know that there are other large carnivores, or meat eaters, like cheetahs, leopards, and hyenas. However, we don't know how they get along with our lion friends. We'll have to keep an eye on that. We also know that lions eat plant-eating animals, like Mike stated, and that we missed the rainy season and are starting into the dry season, which would be their winter."

"Well, their winter is certainly different from ours," replied Lydia.

"Yes," stated Dora. "But just like Michigan, the plant life will die or go *dormant* during winter even though it is not cold. That means the *herbivores*, or plant-eaters, will have to move to find more food. I assume our lions will follow them. Perhaps we'll see that."

"Well, time to start out again," said Mike. He fluttered his wings and flew out of the covering of the tree.

Suddenly, a yellow bird with a black head squawked and dove at him from the left.

"Mike!" screamed Lydia.

"Aaaaahhhhhh!" yelled Mike. He took a quick dive to the right and flew down and out over the grassland.

"Oh no!" yelled Lydia. "Quick, Dora, we need to distract the bird."

The bird was hungry and right on Mike's tail. If Mike flew left, the bird flew left. If Mike flew right, the bird flew right. Dora and Lydia knew Mike could fly faster than the bird, but they were not sure if he would tire before the bird would. The bird was relentless, though Mike was clever and kept swooping and circling, never flying straight so that the bird could not gain speed on him. Speed was his friend when trying to escape a bird, because dragonflies are usually faster than birds.

Dora and Lydia quickly discussed a plan, and they were off.

"Mike, fly this way!" yelled Dora.

Mike heard and headed their way. The girls rushed at the bird, and Mike flew straight between them. The bird had a slightly swooping, fast and direct flight pattern. It also had a long, strong bill with which to eat insects. Lydia's eyes widened as she neared the bird, praying their plan would work.

She and Dora passed Mike and headed for either side of the bird. With one dragonfly on the left and one on the right, the bird got confused and paused in its flying. That was all the girls needed. They bumped the bird on the sides of its head and then flew over him and in opposite directions. By this time Mike was safely hidden on a nearby tree branch. Dora and Lydia safely made it to separate trees as well and watched to see if the bird was following either of them. The bird swooped toward Lydia and then turned and flew away.

After a few minutes when they were sure the bird was gone for good, Dora and Lydia joined Mike in his tree. Hugs were given all around, and they thanked God for saving them.

Dora pulled out her laptop and looked up the description of the bird. "Here it is!" she cried. "A Black-Headed Oriole. They eat insects, caterpillars, locusts, and beetles. But they'll also eat fruits, berries, and nectar. That information could help us should we ever see one again."

"If we ever see one again, it will be too soon!" said Mike. "And thanks for saving me."

"What are friends for?" Lydia smiled.

CHAPTER 7

PRIDE LIFE

Rrrroooooaaaaarrrrrr!

The branch Lydia, Dora, and Mike were resting on rumbled from the close proximity of the roar of Jones.

"Uh-oh," said Mike. "Sounds like Jones is upset."

"Let's go check it out," said Dora.

The three dragonflies left their perch on the branch and headed over to where the lions had been resting most of the day. As they came closer, they saw what the problem was. Two bachelor males had stumbled into Jones's territory and came up to his pride of lions. He roared and stood tall with his teeth bared, as if daring them to come any closer.

They stopped in their tracks and seemingly weighed their options. Jones was a very large lion. He was about four feet tall and eight feet long, weighing in at five hundred pounds. The two intruders should have smelt his scent on the trees and rocks. Either they noticed and wanted to see if they could defeat him and take over the pride, or they just plain didn't notice.

One of the male lions, the smaller of the two, looked down after staring at Jones, a sure sign of surrender. The other one, however, didn't give up so easily. He actually roared back. The dragonfly friends knew that Jones's roar could be heard up to five miles away, because they had heard it themselves. They were not convinced this intruding lion had such a loud roar. Jones roared again, even louder, in response and shook his mane at the unwelcome lions.

The roaring trespasser didn't take the hint. Instead, he crouched low and sprang for Jones's throat.

"Oh no!" shrieked Lydia, hiding her eyes under her wings. "I can't watch."

"Don't worry," consoled Mike. "Jones will beat him. He looks bigger to me."

The fight didn't last long. Jones got the upper hand, so to speak, and the other lion gave up and ran away before he could be injured beyond repair.

Jones shook his mane and roared again for good measure as the two intruders ran away. Then he proudly walked back to where the females were lying. Night was coming, and it was almost time to hunt. Jones lay down to conserve his energy for the hunt.

"Whew, I'm glad that ended well," said Lydia.

"All right," said Dora matter-of-factly. "We need to go back to base camp and organize our notes to be ready for the hunt tonight."

By this time they had been studying the lions for three weeks and had witnessed many a hunt. Most of the time the lions were not successful in their hunts. In fact, according to Dora's calculations, they were successful only about 30 percent of the time. The last few nights had been unsuccessful, so the lions were probably getting quite hungry by this point. Sometimes when they got too hungry, they would steal meat from a cheetah or some other predator who was weaker than they were. Cheetahs were incredibly fast and caught food somewhat easily, but they were not the largest of cats and so gave up their food to stronger predators like the lions or a group of hyenas.

The sun was down, and the lions were stalking. Mike led Lydia and Dora through the moonlight, following the group of lions. The cubs had been left behind, and it was the females that were leading the way. They usually brought down the meat, and then the two males ate first. Then the females ate and after that the cubs. Every lion knew his or her place, and there was rarely fighting, except briefly over food if one of the large cats overstepped their bounds.

"Here they go," Mike whispered. "They've surrounded that pack of zebras. Let's see who goes in for the kill first. My bet's on Africa."

"She is the dominant female," agreed Dora.

Sure enough, Africa led the way, and the pride was able to bring down three zebras quickly. The rest ran away in a hurry.

Lydia never liked this part of their study on the lions. She would have much preferred it if the lions were plant eaters. She sighed and turned her head away as the lions allowed Jones and Hunter first dibs. The males were hungry and ate about forty pounds each. At this rate there wouldn't be any left for the cubs.

Two of the lionesses turned away and started stalking again. This time they came upon an unsuspecting group of gazelles. They were downwind, and the gazelles, who are very fast runners, were not able to all escape. One of them was brought down by the females who immediately dug in. The cubs would have something to eat after all. Lydia was at least grateful for that, though she still detested watching the lions eat.

Dora was busy writing down which lions ate first, which lions were responsible for the kill, and if there were any lions who didn't get to eat. Tonight was a successful night for the lions, and every one of them ate to their fill.

"Well, let's call it a night," said Dora, closing her notebook. "Tomorrow's another day, and we need more notes on the interaction of the cubs with the rest of the pride."

"Does this mean we have enough information on the hunts and we don't have to watch this anymore?" asked Lydia hopefully.

"I think so." Dora nodded.

"Good," Lydia sighed.

Mike patted Lydia on the back. "Won't it be nice someday when the lion lies down with the lamb and there is no more killing?"

"Sure will," agreed Dora and Lydia together.

CHAPTER 8

SAVING HENRY AND BECCA

Mike stretched and fluttered his wings. The light of the morning sun shone brightly, reflecting off the greenish hues on his wings. He fluttered his wings up and down again and looked about for Dora and Lydia. They were nowhere near their campsite in the Tamboti tree. Mike whistled and listened. It was only a few seconds later when the breeze carried an answering whistle back to him. It had come from the north where Mike could see the pride lounging lazily in the grass.

"I'd love to sleep all day like lions," he sighed. "Well, better get a move on it."

Mike paused to eat a quick breakfast. There was a nook in the middle of the tree the dragonflies used for storage. This is where they kept food and a bit of water in a leaf-cup. After eating, Mike headed north toward the lions where he had heard the answering whistle.

It was a *balmly* day, and there was a soft breeze blowing the grasses. Mike chuckled as he flew over the cubs playing by the adult lions. The cubs where batting at the wind-blown grasses as they moved. Mike heard the whistle again and looked over to a nearby tree. On the lowest branch sat his companions. He flew over.

"Aren't they cute?" asked Lydia.

"Very," said Mike. "By the way, have we named them yet?"

"Don't you remember?" asked Dora. "We have a chart with the names of the lions, lionesses, and their cubs."

She pulled the chart up on her laptop and showed Mike.

"Oh, that's right!" he exclaimed. "For whatever reason, I remembered the names of the adults but not the cubs."

"Well, that's probably because we've not taken the time to study the cubs yet," offered Lydia.

"Well, now's our chance," said Dora. "Today we're watching the cubs and how they interact with their environment and the rest of the pride."

"Sounds good," said Mike. "Well, they are certainly more interesting to watch during the day than the adults."

"Yes, they're very playful," Lydia chuckled.

"Look at Africa's cubs," she continued. "That's Henry," she said, pointing to a darker cub about six months old."

"And that's his sister Becca," added Dora, pointing to a cub the same size, only lighter.

"They sure are adventurous," said Mike. "They're wandering much farther away from the pride than the other cubs."

They were indeed, and it had Lydia concerned after a while. The twin brother and sister cub had chased each other so far away from their mother that they would have to smell their way back to where they began, or Africa, their mother, would need to come looking for them.

Suddenly Mike noticed movement off to the left of the wandering cubs. "Ssshhhh," he hushed Lydia and Dora. "I think I see something."

All three dragonflies looked to the spot where Mike had seen movement. A grey-brown, speckled head with large ears peered over the grasses at the cubs playing nearby.

"Oh no," whispered Mike. "Hyenas!"

The word sent a shudder through Lydia. Her wings rippled from the effect.

"We have to do something," said Dora.

"We have to save them," agreed Mike. "This is what we'll do..."

He quickly laid out his plan, and the three dragonflies flew toward the cubs. Mike zipped over Henry's head, while Lydia zoomed over Becca. Dora kept watch over the hyenas. Mike and Lydia kept close enough to the cubs to keep their attention yet always stayed out of reach of their swatting paws. The cubs liked chasing the dragonflies, and slowly, Mike and Lydia lured Henry and Becca back toward the lounging lionesses and safety.

Suddenly, Dora zipped up to them, yelling, "The hyenas have started toward them and at a quick pace. I think they're going to try and take them out before they reach the pride."

"Oh no!" Mike moaned. "We have to be quick. Come on, Lydia! Lure them faster, and Dora, you go and awaken Africa. Bother her until she stands up!"

Dora knew it would be dangerous to bother the napping lion, but she also knew she had to try. Quickly she flew to Africa and buzzed and flitted around her until Africa was so annoyed she stood up and roared. It was just what the dragonflies were hoping for. The hyenas were only about twenty feet from the cubs when the roar sounded. They stopped in their tracks and sniffed the air cautiously.

That was all the time Mike and Lydia needed. They were still luring the cubs closer to the pride, and as the hyenas paused, they got them within sight of the nearest lioness. Henry and Becca noticed their whereabouts and happily ran to find their mother.

The hyenas gave up and sauntered away.

"Mission accomplished!" Mike beamed, giving high-fives to Dora and Lydia.

"Thank You, Lord," whispered Lydia in a grateful prayer.

The rescuing had been dangerous but well worth it. The cubs were safe and so were the three dragonflies.

CHAPTER 9

A NEW GENERATION

The next week went by smoothly with little interruption. There was one night where the hyenas had Jones surrounded. He roared, and though that didn't scare off the hyenas, it did bring Hunter and two lionesses running. They helped fight off the hyenas. It would only be a matter of time before Jones would no longer be the dominant male in the pride. Either the hyenas would get him and he would be unable to escape, or he would grow too old and weak, and another male would take his place.

There hadn't been a challenge from other males in several weeks now, but even Hunter could probably take on Jones if he tried, which he possibly would do at some point.

The dragonflies noted all of this, as well as kept careful record of hunting successes and failures and the growth and development of the cubs.

It was toward the end of the week after Henry and Becca were saved that two lionesses went into labor. Rachel and Cassandra both dragged themselves off to a private place to give birth. The dragonflies split up. Lydia took up residence near Cassandra, Dora took notes regarding Rachel, and Mike kept an eye on the rest of the pride.

Cassandra did not have too much difficulty. She found a spot among some bushes, well hidden from view, and brought forth four new babies. There were two females and two males. Lydia noted everything that occurred with great delight. Cassandra immediately began licking her cubs to clean them off. She would grab them by the scruff of their necks and lick them with her rough tongue. Then she set them to nursing. The cubs were very small. Lydia estimated them to be between two and four pounds each. Their eyes were closed, and they whimpered softly in their throats at their mother.

On the other side of the pride, Rachel had found a spot among thick grasses hedged in by a rocky area to her back in which to give birth. She was sheltered well. Her labor was a bit more *grievous* and lasted into the night. It was dark by the time all three cubs were out. Dora breathed a sigh of relief when the last cub came out, and Rachel grabbed it by the back of its neck with her teeth. She put it between her paws and set to cleaning it off. The other two cubs were drinking their mother's sweet milk by the time the last cub started getting cleaned off.

The cubs grew quickly, but it was another four weeks before Rachel introduced her new cubs to the pride and another two weeks after that before Cassandra brought her cubs to meet the other members of their extended family. Jones sniffed each cub, and sensing they were his offspring, he allowed them to stay.

The cubs learned hunting skills by chasing tails and each other. The adults were generally patient with them, and the cubs continued receiving nourishment from their mothers. Dora noted that most cubs actually drank their mother's milk until they were about six to eight months old, even though they ate meat at six weeks old. It was a good thing too, because not much meat was usually left for the cubs after a hunt, so the milk supplemented their diet.

It was about this time that Lia's two male cubs, Pounce and Springer, were shooed away from the pride by Jones. Dora estimated the young lions to be a little over three years of age. Lia's cubs were older than the rest of the cubs in the pride, and it was time for her to be pregnant again. Jones took that opportunity to get rid of the two brother cubs so they would not be a threat to his dominance later. Females were always allowed to stay, because they posed no threat to the male leader of the pride.

One afternoon Lydia was lazily resting on a branch of their Tamboti tree when Dora came back from studying the lions.

"Well," she began, "I think we have all the information we need."

"What do you mean?" asked Lydia.

"I mean, I think our study is done here."

"Done? Like we have to go home now?" Lydia's eyes got bigger than normal, and a tear started to form in the corner of one of them.

"But," she continued, choking back the tears, "I've grown so fond of these lions and of Africa. I don't want this study to end."

Mike came flying back at that point. "What's going on?" he questioned.

"Dora says our study is done and it's time to go home," said Lydia, now freely letting the tears flow.

Mike patted her back, and Dora came and gave her a hug. Mike hugged the both of them.

"I know," said Dora. "Let's think of a good way to say good-bye."

"Good-bye would be nice," agreed Lydia, calming down a bit. "It's just that I feel like we have gotten to know these lions, and I feel somewhat responsible for them."

"We're not God," said Mike. "We can't be responsible for them. We've done what we can here, and now we leave them in God's hands. They've always been there anyway."

"I think you've gotten wiser hanging around us," Dora joked.

"So how do we say good-bye?" asked Lydia.

The three friends huddled together and discussed their options.

CHAPTER 10

JOURNEY HOME

"I've got it!" said Mike. "We'll give one more chase to the cubs! Their fun will be our good-bye present to the whole pride."

"Excellent idea," agreed Dora and Lydia.

It was a few hours before nightfall, so the three dragonflies decided to do it then so they could leave early in the morning. They also needed to get word to the termites in the area of their need for transportation to the ocean. So they headed out to find the newest cubs and treat them to some games.

Mike wanted to get the cubs' attention by roaring at them. He wanted to see how loud a dragonfly could roar. Dora thought that was hilarious. They flew above the cubs, and Mike let out his best roar. Evidently, it wasn't loud enough, because the cubs didn't even look up. However, when the three dragonflies roared together, their roar was loud enough to make one of the cubs raise his head and look around briefly.

"Okay," said Mike. "I give up on the roaring. Let's just get them to chase us."

They were having fun with the young cubs, allowing the cubs to get close, but not too close as the cubs chased, jumped, and pounced, trying to catch the dragonflies. The adults watched with lazy eyes at the fun.

Suddenly, there was a flash of yellow and black that zoomed past Lydia.

"Mike!" she screamed. "The oriole's back!"

Mike and Dora came flying toward Lydia as she dodged the oriole's strong bill. They forgot all about the young cubs, who did not forget that they were playing a game of chase with the long-winged insects. The introduction of a fast-moving black-and-yellow bird only proved to intrigue the little lions even more. Now there was another toy to catch, as far as they were concerned.

Lydia zipped left and right and up and down. Mike and Dora tried to distract the bird until Mike finally noticed out of the corner of his eye that the cubs were trying to swat the bird. That gave him an idea. He zoomed closer to Lydia and yelled at her to dive toward the cubs.

Quickly Lydia dove down, taking the trailing bird with her. It was just what one of the cubs was waiting for. In a crouched position, the little lion waited until the oriole was within reach, and then he pounced. That was the end of the oriole and the end of the game for the three dragonflies. Gratefully, they quickly flew back to their Tamboti tree and hunkered down in a crevice so as not to be seen by any more hungry birds.

"That was close," said Lydia, letting out a sigh. "Thank you both for helping me."

"Not a problem," Mike smiled. "Now, how about we get word to those termites so we can leave for home early tomorrow?"

"I'm not going back out there," said Lydia.

"I'll do it," said Mike. "I'm not afraid. Besides, our little lion friends took care of that pesky bird."

"Do you know where the termite mound is from here?" asked Dora.

"Yes, I remember."

"It shouldn't take you more than twenty minutes to get there and twenty minutes back. If you talk for twenty minutes, you should be back in an hour."

"You've got it down to the minute, eh Dora?" Mike laughed. "I guess I'll be back in an hour."

True to his word, Mike was back in an hour. By that time the girls had gathered up all their belongings and were ready to call it a night. Mike informed them that the plane would be there to fetch them at first light.

The next morning dawned bright and beautiful. Lydia waved at the sleeping pride as the plane flew low over the savannah. She knew they couldn't see her and that they didn't even know they had been the object of study for more than three months, but she waved anyway.

The long ride home was good to reflect on their journey together, and the three dragonflies shared many fond memories. The ride home was also uneventful for the most part. They met up with Bob the termite again and were able to tell him thank you for all his help. Then it was back on the barge. This time they didn't get locked in any rooms.

By the time they reached U.S. soil, they were ready to be home.

"There's the subway station," said Mike.

"The last leg of our journey," added Dora.

They bought their tickets and waited for their train to come. Insects of all shapes and sizes were busy getting on and off the trains, heading here and there.

"It certainly is much busier here than in Africa," noted Lydia.

"That's something I will miss," said Dora. "There was so much time to just watch, take notes, and reflect."

"Well, just because it's busy here doesn't mean we have to be," said Mike. "Let's make an effort to not be too busy but to take that time for reflection and study and fellowship."

"And prayer," added Lydia. "That got us through more than one mess."

They all laughed as their train approached. Their peace and joy continued as they pulled into the train station in Grand Rapids, Michigan.

"Well, here we are," said Dora as they got off the train and headed up to the surface.

"It's good to be back," Mike smiled.

"It'll be exciting to give our report to the AIR at next fall's meeting," said Lydia.

"Yeah, but I'm not getting too close to the fish jumping the ladder in the Grand River. I've had enough run-ins with insect-eating predators.

Lydia and Dora laughed in agreement. It had been an experience to remember, and they would always remember the lions they studied with fondness. They would also always remember and give thanks to God for His protection and that they had a close-up view of His glory revealed in creation.

PRAYER

If you don't know Jesus as your Savior and Lord, if you've never asked Him to live in your heart, now is your chance! Jesus Christ is the only way to heaven, and He wants you to be there with Him when you die or when He comes back to earth, whichever comes first. It is because God loves you and everyone else on earth that He sent Jesus to die for our sins—all the bad things that we have done—so that we wouldn't have to suffer in hell for them. Jesus paid the price for us! If you want Jesus to save you and have His Spirit live in your hearts, pray this prayer from your heart and believe it, and you will be saved!

> Father, I confess that I have sinned. I confess that I need You to save me. I believe Jesus died for my sins, and now I ask You, Jesus, to forgive me for my sins that I may live forever with You. Please send me Your Holy Spirit. Baptize me in Your Spirit and give me the grace to live each day for You. Jesus, be my Savior and the Lord of my life. I love

> You. Help me to grow to know You better, to love You more, and to bring glory to Your name.

Congratulations! The Bible says that angels in heaven rejoice over the decision you have just made! Now you need to be with other believers and read your Bible and pray always. God loves you!

GLOSSARY

Pride: A family of lions, usually consisting of one or two males and several females with and without cubs.
Hold: A place on a ship where things like boxes are stored.
Dominant: Generally the leader of a group. In this case it is the biggest and strongest lion.
Deciduous: A tree with broad leaves.
Scent: Smell.
Savannah: Grassland.
Dormant: A time when plants sort of go to sleep. They don't grow, and they look almost dead.
Herbivores: Plant eaters.
Balmy: Calm.
Grievous: Troubling.

Made in the USA
San Bernardino, CA
01 December 2016